#58 Woodland Hills
Branch Library
22200 Ventura Boulevard
Woodland Hills, CA 91364

JUN 0 8 2020

W9-BON-797

Your names sound in our midst
To Alexander and Philip

Copyright © 2019 Clavis Publishing Inc., New York

Originally published as *Misschien is doodgaan wel hetzelfde als een vlinder worden*
in Belgium and the Netherlands by Clavis Uitgeverij, 2018
English translation from the Dutch by Clavis Publishing Inc., New York

Visit us on the Web at www.clavis-publishing.com.

No part of this publication may be reproduced or stored in a retrieval system,
or transmitted in any form or by any means, electronic, mechanical, photocopying,
recording, or otherwise, without the prior written permission of the publisher,
except in the case of brief quotations embodied in critical articles and reviews.
For information regarding permissions, write to Clavis Publishing, info-US@clavisbooks.com.

Maybe Dying Is Like Becoming a Butterfly written by Pimm van Hest and illustrated by Lisa Brandenburg

ISBN 978-1-60537-494-9 (hardcover edition)
ISBN 978-1-60537-505-2 (softcover edition)

This book was printed in August 2019 at Poligrafia Janusz Nowak SP. Z O.O., Zbożowa 7, 62-081 Wysogotowo, Poland

First Edition
10 9 8 7 6 5 4 3 2 1

Clavis Publishing supports the First Amendment and celebrates the right to read.

Written by Pimm van Hest
Illustrated by Lisa Brandenburg

MAYBE DYING IS LIKE BECOMING A BUTTERFLY

Clavis

XZ
H

Christopher looks at Grandpa.

"Can I take this caterpillar home?"

"Why?" asks Grandpa.

"So I can put him in a jar."

"Hmm . . . I don't know," says Grandpa.

"He might die if you put him in a jar."

"Oh." That thought shocks Christopher.

Grandpa nods.

"Are you going to die, Grandpa?"
"Someday, sweetheart. But I hope not too soon."
"I also hope not, Grandpa.
Who knows when you will die?"

"No one. No one knows."
"Not even Granny?" asked Christopher.
"Not even Granny."

"Will I ever die, Grandpa?"
"What do you think?"
It's quiet for a while.
Christopher thinks about it.

"I guess I will, Grandpa."
"But I'd rather not."
"No," says Grandpa. "That's understandable."

"I would like to know
when I'm going to die, Grandpa."
"Why, sweetheart?"
"Well, before I die,
I can do a lot of nice things."
"Such as?"
"Go to the beach with the whole family.
Or fly in an airplane with you.
Or get a puppy."

"But you don't have to wait until right before you die.
You can do all those things now."
"Oh, yes . . . I guess so."

"Will you die before me, Grandpa?"
"There's a good chance. A very good chance."
"But could I also die before you, Grandpa?"
"There's a small chance. A very small chance."
"But it's possible, right?"
"Yes, it is possible."

"I want to grow up to be just as old as you, Grandpa.
And then die."
"And I would love to be alive
to see you grow old, Christopher. Just as old as I am now."
"Is that possible, Grandpa?"
"No, sweetheart, unfortunately it's not.
I will die before you get that old."

"What happens after death, Grandpa?"
"That's a good question, my boy.
Hmm, I don't know the answer, really.
I've never died before."

"But, Grandpa, where do you think you go after death?"
"I think I'll go to a place where it rains chocolate."
Christopher laughs out loud.
"And what do you think?"
Christopher is quiet.
"I need a little time to think about that, Grandpa."
"I understand, sweetheart.
Perhaps the special thing about death
might be that no one really knows.
That we can each have our own thoughts about it."

"What have other people thought of, Grandpa?"
"All sorts of things, sweetheart.
Some think that there's a heaven.
A place without sadness or war.
Where everything is always fine.
Others think that they will be born again after death.
And each time, you get wiser when you're back on earth.
But there are also people who think that there's nothing after death.
That it feels exactly the same as before you were born."

"Oh," says Christopher.
"I think that I'm going to search for you, Grandpa, when I'm dead."

"Why do you think we die?" Grandpa asks Christopher.
"Because our body is worn out?" Christopher guesses.
"That's right, my boy. And I think," Grandpa continues,
"that we die because dying is part of life.
Everything that lives eventually dies."

"Here's an easier question," says Christopher.
"Why do you think we're born?"
"Hmm. What do you think?"
"Well, I think that we are born
to learn all sorts of things on earth.
And some people learn faster than others. Right?"
Tears fill Grandpa's eyes. He nods.
"You just taught me something very beautiful, sweetheart."

"Are you afraid of dying, Grandpa?"
"Honestly?
Sometimes I am, and sometimes I'm not.
Sometimes I think about it a lot,
and other times I don't think about it at all.
One moment, dying seems scary
and it makes me feel sad.
Another moment it feels peaceful.
It comforts me to know that I will die one day.
Does that sound odd to you?"

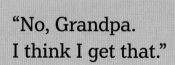

"No, Grandpa.
I think I get that."

"Although, I would miss a lot of things when I'm dead," said Grandpa.
"Like Granny's delicious homemade vegetable soup.
Or twirling snowflakes.
Or laughing at your dad's jokes.
Or sitting on a bench with you in the park.
And so many other things too."

"But maybe you don't have to miss all those things, Grandpa."
"Why is that?"
"Maybe all those things are still there after death."
"Yes," says Grandpa. "You might be right.
Maybe all those things are still just there after death."

Dear Grandpa,

I've been thinking again.
Maybe dying is like changing
into a butterfly.
Do you know why?
Because when the butterfly is there,
the caterpillar is gone.
It seems like the caterpillar is dead.
But it isn't.
It has become a butterfly.

So maybe dying is like
becoming a butterfly.
Maybe you turn into something else,
something you can't think of yet.

Into something beautiful . . .

See you later, Grandpa.

Christopher

Children and Death

By Rebecca Dabekaussen

Sooner or later, everyone has to deal with death in his or her life. Unfortunately, children can't escape this either. Children who are given the space and opportunity to talk about loss, saying goodbye, and death have a head start. Once a child is comfortable talking about feelings of a small loss—such as losing a toy animal, the death of a pet, or a friend moving away—it is easier to talk about a significant loss too, for example when Mommy's very ill, when Grandpa suddenly dies, or a classmate has a fatal accident.

Research shows that it is better to inform children and involve them in a loss or parting.

By being open, you create the opportunity to talk to one another about the situation and how it affects your child. And by listening carefully to him or her, you also strengthen your bond of trust.

It can be difficult to talk about death. You may prefer to protect your child from the great amount of grief that death can cause. However, if you talk to them openly, children will feel less alone with their emotions.

Useful and Guiding Tips to Discuss Death with Children

Start simple. Have a conversation with your child about the fly that lies dead on the windowsill. "Look—it doesn't move anymore. Its body is broken." In this way, your child becomes familiar with talking about death as something that is a part of nature.

It helps children if you stay with the facts. No matter how loving your intentions, don't try to soften death. Do not say, "If you're dead, you're sleeping," but explain how it is: "Grandpa died—his body doesn't work anymore."

Children respond more to what you do and how you appear than to what you say. Before you talk about death or to tell your child bad news, make sure that you yourself are at ease. When your child notices that you are calm, he or she will probably respond (more) calmly as well.

Conversations with children are often very short. Children easily alternate difficult issues with play. If your child suddenly changes the subject during a difficult conversation, it often means that he or she is processing it.

Provide space for emotions. Young children often don't understand questions like "How do you feel at this moment?" A better question is "Can you tell me what you feel in your tummy? Are you feeling sad, angry, happy?" With that, they can sometimes say what they feel. Or simply say what you see: "I see that it makes you sad—am I right?"